BRIDGE OF FATE

A ROAD'S BELOVED SHORT STORY

ERICA ANOE

LONELY ROBOT PRESS

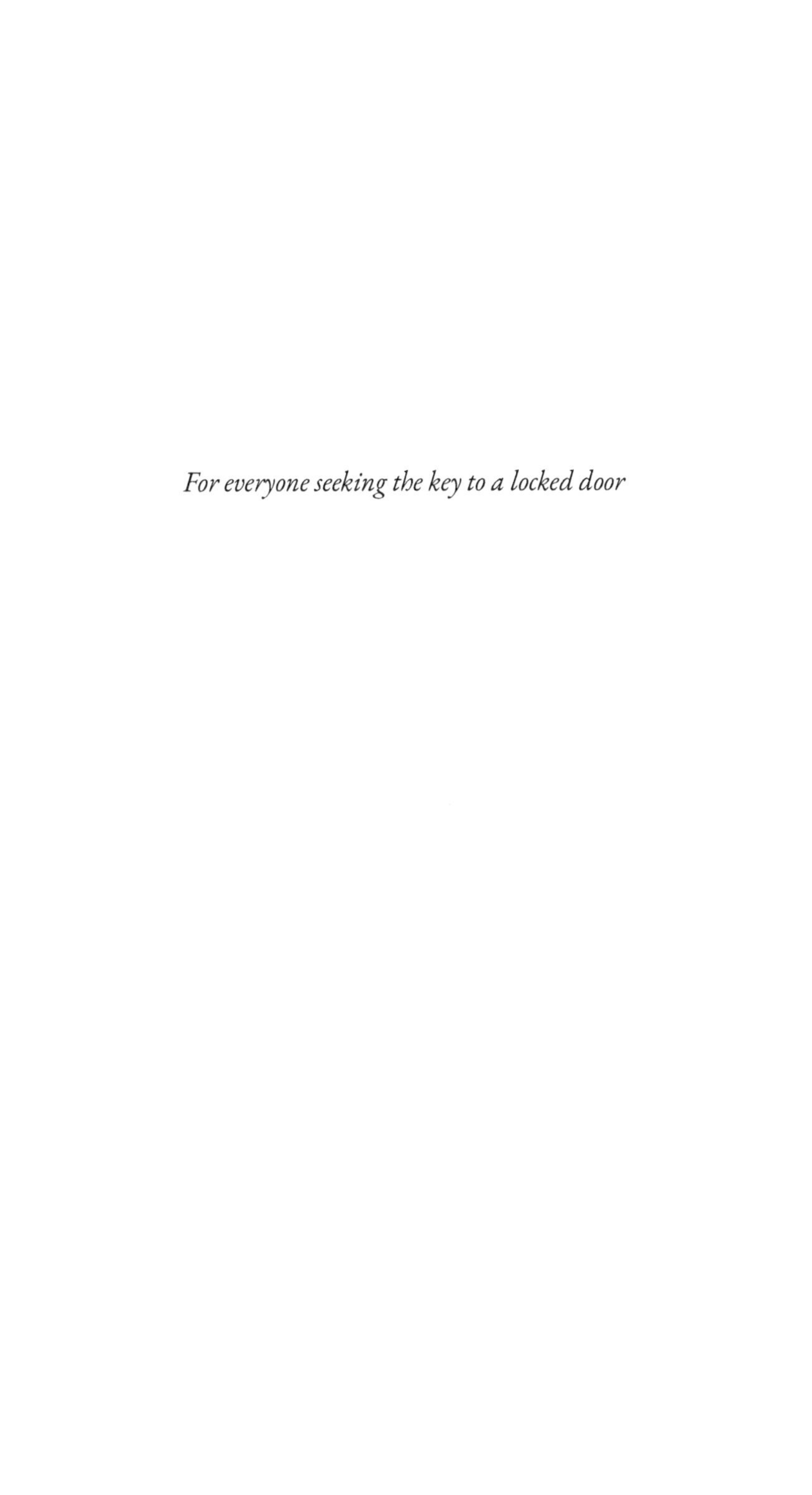

For everyone seeking the key to a locked door

The hardest thing in life is to know which bridge to
cross and which to burn.

— David Russell

ONE

Etta woke from her dream of locked doors. This time she was breathing deep and hard and her skin was damp all over. She'd had the dream every night since becoming Queen of Worldsbridge. Sometimes, it was oddly serene – she walked casually past the locked doors, almost floating, saying to herself *yes, this one is locked*, and then a moment later, *so is this one*.

But this night, she'd been running, rattling the knobs. She'd heard screaming from the other side of some of the doors, while others taunted her with achingly beautiful music. Some doors were hot and some cold. Finally, she'd come upon one with the most gorgeous light slipping through the spaces at the top, bottom and sides of the door. She had tried to find a crack large enough to peer through – lying on the floor, attempting to stand on the doorknob – and yet no position, no matter how contorted, allowed her to see anything more. Her curiosity and desire had overcome her, and Etta had banged on the door and screamed herself hoarse.

She sat up, wiping sweat away with the edge of a quilt far fancier than she was used to. Her lover Piper stirred, flinging one heavily marked arm vaguely in Etta's direction. "What's the matter?" Piper mumbled.

"It's nothing."

Piper sat up, wide awake now. "Look, I may not have much experience with relationships that last more than an hour or two, but I'm pretty sure that when your lover wakes up looking like she just swam for her life to escape a riptide and she does it more nights than not – you're supposed to press for more details when she keeps saying it's nothing."

Etta grinned. "Have you been reading in the library about how people behave?"

"I meet plenty of people when I travel the Road. I know things about people. I know what their secrets are like."

"Then maybe you also know that people don't like to give up their secrets," Etta said.

"Most people I've met are dying to give up their secrets."

Etta sighed and stood, sliding her feet into slippers to shield them against the chill of the stone floor. Cool air made her drying sweat feel icy, and she wrapped herself in a shockingly luxurious robe hanging from a nearby hook and tossed the one beside it to Piper. "Honestly, if you're only going to know someone for an hour or two, secrets burn for release. If you're going to have to look a person in the eye in the morning and explain what you're going to do about your secrets, it's a very different story."

"Really," Piper said, climbing out from under the bedclothes and standing naked, ignoring the robe. She seemed unaffected by the room's temperature aside from the visible tightening of her skin, highlighted by the way it subtly changed the shapes of the birthmarks that wound over nearly every inch of her. "So you're telling me that the better you know someone, the less you tell them?"

Etta shrugged. "I haven't made a study of it, but it seems true right now."

Piper raised an eyebrow. Etta was still as affected by Piper's presence as when they'd first seen each other, and she had an urge to step across the room and distract her from any further desire to ask questions. Piper always seemed to know when Etta felt this way, and she winked. "I could leave the city and come back pretending to be a stranger. I could call myself... Popper?"

Etta grabbed a pillow off the bed and flung it at Piper. It struck her in the chest with a light thump, a few feathers escaping and fluttering to the ground. Etta felt sudden guilt at her lack of care for the finely worked pillow. She was reminded yet again of how quickly and dramatically her circumstances had changed. She wrapped her arms over her chest and squeezed tightly, aware of the marks that were now growing over her body too without having to look at them.

Before Etta noticed her moving, Piper had pulled her close. Despite the time they'd spent together, Piper still smelled of distant places, of dust that Etta had never tasted on her lips. "Come now, we don't know each other well at all. According to your rules, it's too soon to hide things from me."

Etta laughed softly to reward her. Then she tried to find a way to form her strange thoughts and feelings into words. The dreams were only the most obvious part of it. Always since the day she'd met Piper, dreaming or awake, she felt some version of what that dream expressed – the sense that she was separated from many significant things, locked away from something vital. Whether she ignored it blithely or railed against it, the fact of the locks remained – alongside the promise of whatever her dreaming mind conceived of as doors. "Piper, what is the Road? Normally, I mean. I understand that having the Road actually appear to you in human form is rare."

"Yes, that is an unusual way to experience the road – and also not the ordinary way to become a Road's Beloved," Piper agreed.

Etta had joined the ranks of the eternal travelers a few moons ago in just such a rare and dramatic fashion. Until then, she had been a member of the city guard, bound by the world's strict magical divisions between City, Road and Wild. Though she'd worked at the city gate, she could only look out at the world beyond the walls and greet the occasional Road's Beloved who arrived – only a Road's Beloved could cross the magical boundaries that divided the essential components of the world.

She had always wondered what it would be like to step out onto the Road, to embrace the uncertainty of travel, to follow its delineations to whatever destination it pointed toward. Even more daringly, she'd wondered how it would be to leave the Road and wander into the Wild, where, according to the stories, there lived creatures with motivations and powers that humans could barely comprehend. Over many days, Etta had memorized the shape of the road that wound into the distance. She had counted the shrubs that lined it, and, farther in the distance, the trees.

Piper had arrived and seen that curiosity and hunger immediately – and allowed Etta to satisfy it. Etta had been fascinated by Piper not only because she was beautiful and powerful but because of the freedom she represented. She could cross any boundary she wanted, and apparently that included the boundaries of propriety. They'd kissed for the first time within minutes of knowing each other. Etta, sensing that their time was limited but not wanting it to be, had been voracious, eager and unafraid. She'd barely recognized herself, and even in those first moments together, the thought of Piper continuing her journey alone had been devastating.

Piper at first treated Etta as if leaving was inevitable, but she'd offered a compelling consolation prize – the ability, for a limited time, to step out of the city and onto the Road. Etta remembered tripping over her pant legs trying to dress before the magic ended (rather than giving a specific time limit, Piper had said only that Etta would know when she needed to return and would ignore that knowledge at her peril). She'd run to the city gate so quickly her breath began to feel like needles entering her lungs. Then there was the first wonderful step onto the Road.

Despite the barrier she'd always known was present, this first step felt shockingly ordinary. Etta could simply take it, and then another and another. She'd turned back, awestruck, seeing the city wall from the outside for the first time in her life. Though the distance she'd put between herself and the wall was short, and the structure rose well above her head, it seemed small and provincial now that she'd momentarily escaped it.

Before she could do anything else, however, the stranger had taken her by the wrist. She'd felt the marks burning into her at his touch, physical signs of a changing destiny.

Piper touched the spot Etta had been thinking of, the thick black X on the inside of her wrist over the place where the veins came closest to the surface. "The Road is the person you saw, always. Usually, you get to know that person slowly, revealed in glimpses. The unusual part is to see so much at once. But your view's not wrong. You were shown the nature of the Road. You are a Road's Beloved."

Etta looked into Piper's eyes, searching for signs of jealousy or doubt. All she saw was Piper's usual impish expression, and the steadiness beneath that, the quality she was learning to rely on. "How did it happen for you?" she asked Piper.

"I was born to the Road," Piper said. "The birthmarks have been on me as long as I can recall."

"Were you traveling it always?"

"More or less. My mother was from the Wild and my father from the City. The Road brought them together. All of it designed to make me who I am. Being a Road's Beloved means being touched by fate. You understand that, my Queen." Piper nudged Etta at that, grinning.

"Yes," Etta said. "Fate isn't done with me."

"That's a good thing." Piper looked around the luxurious royal bedroom. "It's working for you so far."

"I can't rest with it, though. That's what *he* did." She thought of Willburn, the mad and twisted king she'd replaced. Sitting still at the crossroads of Worldsbridge had transformed him into a monster, and Etta had no intention of following in his footsteps.

"So this is what you're not telling me," Piper said. "You have some idea of what you're supposed to do and it frightens you." Piper began to pace, muscles rippling as smoothly as a wild creature, her nudity terribly distracting.

Etta shook her head and laughed. "I'm going to have to either take you back to bed or dress you so I can think." She picked up the second robe again and wrapped it around Piper's shoulders. "What do you know of Worldsbridge?"

Piper shrugged, picking at the edges of the robe as if she wasn't sure what to do with it. "This is my first time here. I know what you do. It's a great crossroads. That's what the Road marked on your wrist."

"Remember what Willburn said. He called Worldsbridge the place where all roads meet. *All* roads."

Piper scratched at a coiling pattern on the side of her neck. "He'd gone crazy, Etta. We've explored the roads in and out of this place. In a manner of speaking, *anywhere* is a place where all roads meet."

"I think there's more to Worldsbridge than a manner of speaking." She took Piper's hands and led her to the window. It was dark, but the moon illuminated bits of the road in the distance. "Beyond the walls of the city, everywhere you have walked – is it all the same world?"

"It's a big world."

"But the same one."

"There's Road, City and Wild."

Etta bit her lip, the intensity of her dream making her heart pound when she recalled it. "I think there's more."

Two

Piper found Etta the next day in the library. "I thought we were going to search for villages in the wilds to the north."

Etta looked up from her book, squinting. She stood, stretching, and checked the angle of the sun through the skylight above. "We have time."

"What's so interesting in that book?"

"Pictures," she said. "Look." She held the pages open to Piper.

"I've never seen people who looked like that before." Piper said.

"Exactly. Look at those clothes. And here. This boat. In all your travels, have you seen a shape like this?"

Piper peered at the images. "I can't say that I have." Fear she wasn't used to trickled down her spine.

Etta brushed the back of Piper's knuckles with a finger. "What's the matter?"

"Nothing."

Etta raised an eyebrow. "Someone I know told me you're not supposed to let your lover get away with saying that."

Piper closed the book. "I'm used to walking down a road when I don't know where it's going. I know what it's like to face that. I know what it's like to leave behind everything that makes sense to you, to realize you'll never really know anyone and never stay anywhere." She fell silent and walked slowly once around the library, trailing her fingers over the spines of the books, adjusting their places on the shelves. When she returned to Etta, she took her face in both hands and kissed her hard. "You're turning everything upside down," she said fiercely. "I've stayed with you in a way I've never done before, but at the same time – I think you're about to take away the one familiar thing I took for granted." She gestured in a way intended to encompass everything – or what until recently she'd thought was everything. "It never occurred to me that I might even have to leave this world. I never even dreamed something like that could be possible."

"How are you so sure you'd be the one to leave?"

Piper shrugged. "Maybe you'd leave too. I don't know what the Road wants for you. But I can tell you that as long as I've lived, if there's an unknown path to take, the Road wants me on it. I can feel it in my bones. If you find a door and open it, I'll have to go through it."

A shadow passed over Etta's expression, but the determination on her face didn't ease. She stroked the book absently with one hand. Piper sat on the table and took it from her. She wasn't used to the indoor smells around her – the paper, the candle wax. Normally, she made a point of leaving quickly, long before she learned to want to stay. Worldsbridge, though, offered the greatest temptation to stay she'd ever experienced in the form of Etta, and, if Etta's suspicions were correct, the Road was going to ask more of her here than it ever had before. Not for the first time since arriving here, she felt a flash of sympathy for the mad King Willburn. If he'd suspected the same things Etta did, if he'd sensed, as Piper did, the Road pulling him eternally, even beyond the world itself – at this point, Piper could understand why he'd sat down on the crossroads and refused to move again.

"Piper," Etta said, "I have to know."

Piper laughed softly. She'd always been the one who understood how things worked. The undeniable pull of the Road defined her life. Now, she was at the mercy not only of the Road, but also of this woman and her books. Sensing that her time – with Etta, in Worldsbridge and in the world she knew – was running out, she shoved herself to her feet. "Let me know when you're ready to walk north."

Three

Etta woke from her dream of locked doors full of resolve. Beside her, Piper snored, and Etta turned toward her with regret. She'd had time to memorize the lines of Piper's face, and she knew she would never forget it. Gently, careful not to wake her lover, she pressed her nose to Piper's hair and breathed in the scents of distant cities, mingled with the stranger scents of the wild. Food she didn't know, plants and animals she'd never seen. She shivered, then tore herself away.

It was clear that Piper didn't want to leave the world she knew, and Etta could understand that. Piper had lived a life of leaving. Born to the Road, she'd said, in a way that made it sound like she'd never known a home. She'd been finding one at Worldsbridge, and Etta paused to recall her childhood and its comforts, the balm of familiarity.

On the other hand, what Etta needed was to leave. She wanted to escape this city, to cross borders that had always been closed to her. She eased herself out of the bed.

She'd gone to the library to look for books and maps, but she'd met the Road and should have known better than to believe dried ink on dead trees. Etta's flesh was the map and the way and the key. It wasn't a matter of finding how to reach another world, it was a matter of being willing to. Etta was Queen of Worldsbridge now, and the city would give its secrets to its Queen if she truly wanted them.

Etta's life as a city guard had taught her all the obvious ways in and out of the city, so she did not go to those places now. Instead, she went to the throne room, where the mad King Willburn had spent many frozen years. That spot was the true Crossroads, it was where the manifested Road had led her, and it was where that being had disappeared. She knew it had to hold the secret.

The way to the throne room was less dusty than it had been when Willburn ruled. Etta had ordered windows opened and hallways aired, and cool night air toyed with her hair as she walked past ancient portraits and suits of armor. She looked at the eyes of the men and women who'd been rulers of this place before her. What had they known? What had they hidden?

She could never walk into the throne room without a shiver. It had been forbidden for most of her life, and she still couldn't quite believe the domain now belonged to her.

The great doors opened silently, and Etta slipped inside. The windows of the room aligned perfectly with the cardinal directions. The ceiling above arched majestically, held up with many great beams that must have been cut from unimaginably tall trees. "What did you know, Willburn?" Etta murmured. "What frightened you?"

There was a door here somewhere, and all she needed was to step through.

Four

Piper woke to a cooling bed. She knew immediately that Etta hadn't simply slipped away for a walk. She pushed away the covers and slapped at the top of her left thigh, where her birthmarks were burning. She fumbled her way to a candle, lit it and glanced down at her body.

The body of a Road's Beloved was a living map, the Road had explained. She'd noticed changes in her markings before – they were an ever-changing record of every Road she had ever and would ever walk, and sometimes the turns she took and decisions she made shifted them. However, she'd never seen them shift before her eyes as they were doing now. She'd never known how to read the patterns of the Roads depicted on her body before she walked them, but this time she didn't need to read them to know what they meant. She cursed under her breath and headed for the throne room, where she was sure she'd find Etta.

FIVE

It was the floor, Etta decided. She stared at the patterns formed by the places the flagstones met and thought she recognized shapes she'd seen on Piper's body. She walked over the lines as if over a tightrope, toe to heel and heel to toe. "Open for me," she said to the Road. "Whatever you opened for Willburn, whatever he refused, open it for me. I won't say no."

She followed one line after another, back and forth across the throne room. The path she followed seemed longer than possible. It should have crossed over itself, and yet it had not. Etta recalled something Piper had told her when they first met – that every step she'd ever taken was new. Gradually, she realized that there was more light in the throne room than there should have been, and the light was of a quality she didn't recognize, as if it had come from a brighter sun.

She remembered the light she'd seen in her dream, the one that she'd felt nearly desperate to reach. Etta's heart began to pound. She stretched her arm forward. The details of the throne room seemed foggy now, her fingers brighter and more vivid under the emerging sun. She thought she saw water glinting in the distance.

A distant sound caught her attention, and she paused in her journey. Piper's voice called her name, very faintly. "Piper," she called back, "it's beautiful. Come with me."

Six

Piper could barely see Etta. The entire throne room was filled with strange light. She wanted to run back to the comfortable and luxurious bedroom – or even to the familiar road just outside the city. But Piper had not become who she was by going backward when the Road urged her onward. She took a deep breath and ran toward Etta, blinded by the light.

She ran farther than should have been possible within the throne room, until her muscles ached. She realized she was stumbling and, looking down, saw her feet plunging into sand within each step. She slowed and stopped, realizing she was alone.

Piper stood on a beach of pristine sand. An ocean she didn't know rolled to her west. The sun seemed to lean on her shoulders, its weight heavier than she was used to. In the distance, a great mountain scraped the sky, wisps of smoke emerging from its summit. She called for Etta – screamed for Etta – but in her heart she already knew the truth.

She prided herself on leaving well before it was time. This time, she'd resisted, and the Road had taken matters into its own hands. Going back was never really an option, but this time, she couldn't even have pointed in the direction that would take her back. Like it or not, she'd crossed through Worldsbridge and into one of the other worlds Etta had believed were possible. She looked out toward the water and saw a boat very like the picture Etta had shown her.

Piper thought of Etta's quick smile and her powerful but gentle hands. They'd had longer together than she was used to, long enough to start to learn each other's rhythms. It ached to think of it, and Piper suspected she would feel the loss for a long time to come.

Wherever she stood, there was no obvious Road to speak of, but she found the next step and took it.

SEVEN

Etta looked around for Piper but didn't see her. She took a step, then another and another. She saw a Road, a bridge ahead of her. It glowed with promise, and she ran across it eagerly. But as she reached the other side, she felt an unmistakable sense of familiarity. The sun was different, she was sure of it, but she knew the contours of the road she walked, and she knew the wall ahead. She recognized the skyline of the city in the distance.

"No," she whispered. "It can't be." She sped her steps until she reached the city gate and the guard tower there.

The group of people waiting for her didn't contain anyone she recognized. They wore armor made of different materials, carried spears tipped with metal rather than bone. She looked from side to side, both seeking a face she knew and afraid to find one.

A woman stepped away from the group and removed a feathered helmet. The shape of her eyes seemed unusual to Etta. The woman knelt before her.

"My Queen, we are honored to welcome you here," she said.

Etta was afraid to ask, but she had to know. "Where exactly is here?" she asked.

"Worldsbridge, of course," the strange woman said. "Your city, where you rule."

"Has a Road's Beloved arrived here recently?" Etta asked, still looking about as if Piper might appear at any moment.

"Not for a long time other than you. We are eager to hear your news of other worlds."

Etta felt a flutter of fear in her chest, but then she stroked the thick X on the inside of her wrist. The crossroads. Worldsbridge, which seemed to be her world. The Road had carried Piper elsewhere, and perhaps it would see fit to reunite them somewhere around a future bend. In the meantime, Etta stepped into the city, ready to explore the next facet of her realm.

Author's Note

When I wrote the first Road's Beloved story, "Queen of the Crossroads," I was not prepared for how often Piper would wend her way into other stories. She's already shown me that she will travel over land and sea, across time and through different worlds, and soon enough, if you care to join her, you'll see it too. However, though Piper initially treated Etta carelessly, it also became clear that she never forgot her Queen, that meeting Etta was a turning point for her, and that Piper after Etta guards the hearts of her lovers and always remembers what Etta taught her.

Because of this, I realized I needed to know more about what happened while Piper and Etta were together and what made them part – at least for now. The exhilarating thing I've found about writing is that if I have a question about my characters, the best way to find the answer is to tell another story. When I do that, surprises are always in store, and I learn more than I initially set out to find.

While it's bittersweet for me that Piper and Etta aren't together at the end of this story, the consolation is that Etta has so much more to do. Like Piper, I initially conceived of

Etta as a throwaway character. At first she was, "the guard who blushed." Of course, she became much more than that in "Queen of the Crossroads," and in "Bridge of Fate" she has begun to truly come into her own. Etta taught Piper – and by extension, me – that there are no throwaway characters, only people whose full potential hasn't yet been revealed.

I'm endlessly curious about the future of the Road's Beloved, as well as what bridges Etta will find and cross from here. Thank you for walking beside Etta and Piper, and beside me, as we travel these unknown Roads together.

– Erica Anoe, February 2022

Acknowledgments

The first thank you is always to you for reading.

Thank you to Elizabeth for always being willing to have a conversation about Etta and Piper, for checking over this story for errors and for creating a beautiful cover that gets to the heart of what this story and Worldsbridge are about.

Thank you to Lonely Robot Press for creating a beautiful edition of this story.

Thank you to Dean Wesley Smith for being my deadline. Without you, I may not have ever gotten around to actually writing about the Road's Beloved, and my life would be poorer for it. Without your challenges, I would never have written so much about the Road's Beloved so quickly. It's made for a lot of late nights, but I'll be the first to say that late nights with Piper can be some of the best.

Thank you to Paul for reminding me to treat my writing as important, and for backing that up by understanding how doing that plays out in our lives.

Thank you to the Road and every unknown path and turn I've taken, with my feet or otherwise. It can be scary to move forward without knowing where I'm going, but the paths I have to walk with a flashlight seem to be the most rewarding.

About the Author

Erica Anoe is a hapa haole writer who is interested in exploring characters and places that exist on the borderlands. Born in Kailua, Hawai'i, she currently lives on the mainland and works in cybersecurity.

ALSO BY ERICA ANOE

COMING SOON

Hawaiian Football Blues: A Road's Beloved Short Story

Piper's next adventure is an urban fantasy set in the seedy underbelly of 1970s Hawaii. Visit Lonely Robot Press for more information.

ALSO IN THE ROAD'S BELOVED SERIES

Queen of the Crossroads

Piper is a Road's Beloved, an eternal traveler who has been given power and destiny by the Road itself. The tangle of birthmarks that cover her skin represent the gifts of every road she has ever walked or will ever walk. They are the source of her magic, and they define her place in the world.

When Piper arrives at Worldsbridge to claim a message from its ruler, she expects a simple encounter. Instead, she finds herself threatened by a bitter king who holds secret grudges against her kind.

To survive, Piper must uncover the true nature of Worldsbridge and learn what the Road expects of those it loves.

"Queen of the Crossroads" is a Road's Beloved short story set in the legendary city of Worldsbridge.

HISTORICAL FICTION

Trapped in the Hold of the SS Madras: A Kingdom of Hawai'i Short Story

"We were not sick with smallpox, but we knew we would be soon if we couldn't get out of this hold."

April 1883. The SS Madras arrives at the port of Honolulu with hundreds of workers for the rice paddies of Waikiki – but it also carries smallpox. Historical fiction set in the waters of the Kingdom of Hawai'i, "Trapped in the Hold of the SS Madras" tells the story of a steamer mired in uncertainty, a kingdom determined to avoid another plague, and passengers desperate to disembark before they contract a deadly disease.

Includes a historical note by the author with information about the case heard by the Supreme Court of the Kingdom of Hawai'i that inspired this story.